Maxine is moving up . . .

"Maxine, I've spoken to Mr. Morgan about you," said Diana.

"Is something wrong?" I asked uneasily.

"No, not at all," Diana said with a smile. "You are doing really well with your riding! I know we would all miss you, but I've asked Mr. Morgan to put you in an intermediate group for the second half of camp."

I didn't know what to say. I had never expected to become an intermediate this summer! "But I don't know if—" I began.

"You don't think you're good enough?" Diana interrupted. "You're *more* than good enough. I don't want you to hold yourself back by staying in a beginners group."

As Diana walked away, I tried to figure out why I was upset. I *could* keep up with the intermediates—I was sure of it. But leave our group? Leave my friends? That was the last thing I wanted!

Don't miss any of the books in
this fabulous new series!

#1 *Jessie Takes the Reins*
#2 *Pam's Trail Ride Adventure*
#3 *Maxine's Blue Ribbon*

And look for this other great series
from HarperPaperbacks:

Ballet School

#1 *Becky at the Barre*
#2 *Jillian On Her Toes*
#3 *Katie's Last Class*
#4 *Megan's Nutcracker Prince*

PONY CAMP

Maxine's Blue Ribbon

SUSAN SAUNDERS

HarperPaperbacks
A Division of HarperCollins*Publishers*

This is a work of fiction. The characters, incidents, and dialogues are products of the author's imagination and are not to be construed as real. Any resemblance to actual events or persons, living or dead, is entirely coincidental.

HarperPaperbacks *A Division of* HarperCollins*Publishers*
10 East 53rd Street, New York, N.Y. 10022

Copyright © 1994 by Daniel Weiss Associates, Inc., and Susan Saunders

Cover art copyright © 1994 Daniel Weiss Associates, Inc.

Produced by Daniel Weiss Associates, Inc., 33 West 17th Street, New York, New York 10011.

First printing: October 1994

Printed in the United States of America

HarperPaperbacks and colophon are trademarks of HarperCollins*Publishers*

10 9 8 7 6 5 4 3 2 1

*To Heidi, who introduced me
to Hillcrest Stables.*

Maxine's
Blue Ribbon

"One-two-three, one-two-three . . . Good, Maxine—you've got a nice, smooth canter going. Now pull back on the reins a little . . . ease up . . . pull . . . ease up," Diana Kirk said. "Winnie's head is lowering, she's slowing down . . ."

Diana teaches riding, and she was talking to me, Maxine Brown. Winnie is the horse I ride at Horizon Hills Pony Camp.

"Good stop. Excellent riding, Maxine!" Diana said.

"Thanks," I answered, patting Winnie's neck.

1

It feels great when you turn out to be good at something you really like. And I *love* riding!

"Okay, Peter, let's see your canter," Diana said.

Peter Brody nudged his horse, Hogan, with his knees. They moved into the center of the outdoor ring.

There are three other kids in my Horizon Hills beginners group. Peter Brody is a fifth grader from Jamestown. He's a little plump—I think his parents made him come to pony camp for the exercise. But he's starting to really like riding.

Jessie Johnson rides a horse named Ranger, and Pam Werner rides Gracie. Jessie and Pam and I will all be fourth graders at Westbrook Elementary in the fall. We're almost exactly the same age, too. Jessie's birthday and mine are just a week apart. Pam's is only three weeks later.

Jessie is great at sports, and she's been crazy about horses all her life. Even though she's new to riding, she's catching on fast. Pam only signed up at Horizon Hills because of Jessie—they've been best friends forever. Pam says big animals scare her. But the more Pam rides, the better she likes it, too!

What I like best about this summer—besides riding, that is—is that Jessie, Pam, and I are getting to be friends. And I hope we'll still be friends when school starts again.

The three of us were all at Westbrook Elementary for third grade, too. But we weren't friends then. I haven't had any real friends in a long time . . . like maybe ever?

You see, my dad was in the Air Force until he retired last fall. We had to move every time he got transferred. I'd just about get used to a new bunch of kids, and we would move again.

After a while, I stopped talking to new kids. I knew I'd only have to move again anyway, so why bother? But by the time we ended up here, I didn't have a clue how to make the Westbrook kids like me.

I didn't dress the same way they did. I didn't say the right stuff. And I wasn't good at sports, either—I'd never lived in one place long enough to learn how to play *anything*.

I pretended I didn't care when nobody wanted to talk to me at Westbrook Elementary. Or sit near me at lunch. Or choose me for teams. Or ask me to out-of-school parties. But I did care—plenty.

Since I wasn't hanging around with anyone, I never had much to do on the weekends. In the spring, my mom and dad signed me up for riding lessons—two hours every Saturday afternoon at Horizon Hills Farm.

I thought Mom and Dad were just trying to find something for me to do. No one could have been more amazed than I was when I turned out to be good at a sport!

Of course, a lot of the credit for that goes to Winnie. She's a wonderful horse. She's a beautiful color—a nice, soft gray, with a darker gray mane and tail. She's just the right size for me, not too tall, with neat little ears. And she never loses her temper, even when I do something dumb.

I liked riding so much that I asked my parents if I could go to pony camp at Horizon Hills this summer. Pony camp means riding every day!

Horizon Hills isn't in Westbrook. It's outside of Jamestown, the next town over. I thought I wouldn't have to worry about running into kids from my school.

So my stomach absolutely flip-flopped when I saw Jessie and Pam standing in the barn on the first day of pony camp. I mean, Jessie and Pam are just about the most popular girls at Westbrook Elementary.

And I was sure they thought I was the biggest loser. Jessie always looked frustrated when she watched me in gym at school. She was so good at sports, and I was so bad. I knew she thought I would be just as bad at riding as I was at baseball and soccer.

After a few days, though, Jessie and Pam must have decided that I wasn't going to hold anyone back. And by the end of the first week, we were starting to talk.

Pretty soon, the three of us were hanging around together outside of camp. We went to the mall on weekends, and to Burger Palace, and to the movies a couple of times. And I learned some things that surprised me!

Jessie told me that she always thought I was stuck up, because I wouldn't talk to anybody at school. She hadn't realized that I was just scared I would say something stupid.

"We thought you were too prissy for sports, too," Pam had added. "Like you didn't want to get dirty."

"Then we saw how good you were at riding. I was afraid you would act like a show-off," Jessie went on. "I hate show-offs."

"But you didn't," Pam said.

"Yeah, you were okay," Jessie agreed.

Can you believe it? And I never had any idea that they thought I was a snob.

I was even more careful about what I did and said around Pam and Jessie after that—if I messed up by *not* talking, just think how much I could mess up by saying the wrong thing! I tried to plan everything out beforehand.

Like that night, Pam and I would be sleeping over at Jessie's, and going to her birthday party on Saturday. So while Jessie and Pam took their turns cantering in the outdoor ring for Diana, I thought hard. I thought about the party, and about the present I had chosen for Jessie, and what we might talk about.

When our lesson was over, Jessie, Pam, and I headed back toward the barn together to unsaddle our horses. That's when Diana stopped me.

"Maxine, I've spoken to Mr. Morgan about you," she said.

"Mr. Morgan?" I asked uneasily.

Mr. Morgan is the owner of Horizon Hills Farm and the head of the pony camp. I couldn't imagine what Diana would have to say to him about *me*.

"Is something wrong?" I asked.

"No, not at all," Diana said with a smile. "Something is *right*. You're doing really well with your riding! I know we would all miss you, but I've asked Mr. Morgan to think about putting you in an intermediate group for the second half of camp."

I didn't know what to say. I had never expected to become an intermediate this summer! "But I don't know if—" I began.

"You don't think you're good enough?" Diana interrupted. "Don't worry, Maxine. You're *more* than good enough for most of our intermediate groups. I don't want you to hold yourself back by staying in a beginners group."

Ahead of me, Jessie and Pam had stopped leading their horses. I could tell that they were trying to hear Diana.

"But . . . but . . ." I tried again. I had a sinking feeling in the pit of my stomach.

Diana waved my words away. "You're just being modest, Maxine. Next week Mr. Morgan will take a look at how you're riding," she said. "And I know that he will agree—you're ready for intermediate!" Diana smiled.

As Diana walked away, I tried to figure out why I was so upset. I *could* keep up with the intermediates—I was sure of it. But leave our group? That was the last thing I wanted!

Jessie and Pam would think I was showing off, I just knew they would. Jessie always gets jealous when someone is better than she is at a sport. She would probably stop speaking to me. And instead of starting fourth grade with some real friends, I would be right back where I started—the dork without anybody!

So when I caught up with Jessie and Pam,

I didn't tell them about moving to an intermediate group. Jessie asked, "What did Diana say?"

"Uh . . . nothing much," I mumbled. "She was giving me some tips on holding my reins tighter."

"Diana is a terrific teacher," Pam said.

"Yes, she is," I agreed.

On the one hand, I was glad that I hadn't told them what Diana really said. On the other hand, it isn't right to fib to your friends.

And somewhere, way back in my mind, a tiny voice was saying: "It might have been fun to start doing some of the things intermediates are doing. Like trotting over poles on the ground. Even jumping!"

But I pushed those thoughts away. Friends are more important than anything else. And I would do anything to keep my friends!

"So, what *did* Diana tell you about reining?" Jessie asked as we reached the barn.

Luckily, before I had to come up with something, a man's voice boomed out: "Campers! May I have your attention?"

It was Mr. Morgan. He was standing on an overturned bucket in the middle of the alley that runs through the horses' stalls. All the kids gathered around him to hear his announcement—whenever Mr. Morgan wanted our attention, he always had something fun planned.

"Next week, you will all start practicing for our first horse show and gymkhana. Please remind your parents that it is just two weeks away, at ten o'clock on Friday morning. I know they won't want to miss it."

Peter groaned loudly behind us. "Great—my parents can come see me look like a total jerk on a horse," he said.

"No way," Jessie told him. "We're going to win every blue ribbon in sight. All it takes is a little practice. We'll all work together—we'll be the best group ever!"

Peter smiled, but I felt even worse. If I did well in the next two weeks, I would probably get pushed into an intermediate group. My friends might be the best group ever, but I wouldn't be part of it.

That afternoon Mrs. Johnson picked up Jessie, Pam, and me at the barn at Horizon Hills. We rolled down the winding road toward the highway, past the outdoor riding rings.

In the far ring, we could see a girl riding her horse over some low jumps.

"Stop for a second, Mom!" Jessie said. "I think that's creepy Lisa Harris!"

Lisa Harris and her brother, Kevin, are both intermediates. They are also the biggest know-it-alls at Horizon Hills. And Lisa has been rude to almost everybody.

"Jessie, I don't like you to talk like that," said Mrs. Johnson. But she slowed the car.

As we watched, Lisa's horse sailed over the last jump, a single pole about three feet above the ground.

Jessie sniffed. "I don't think she looks so great," Jessie said. "Did you see the way she grabbed her horse's mane when she came down?"

"She was leaning too far forward," I agreed.

Far away, we heard someone clapping.

"Sally Keller," Pam murmured. "Standing near the gate."

Sally Keller is Lisa's best friend—she does everything Lisa tells her to do.

"Lisa always has to have an audience," Jessie said as Mrs. Johnson drove on. "I can't stand that girl. What a show-off!" she added in a low voice.

"All the intermediates think they're hot stuff," Pam added.

There was no way *I* was going to be an

intermediate—that was that! All the way to Jessie's house, I tried to think of ways to change Diana's mind about moving me.

The Johnsons' house is a big wooden two-story. I'd been there a couple of times before, but only for an hour or so—not long enough to see everything. That day, as Jessie led us in from the garage, we passed a large trophy case with a glass front. It was absolutely crammed with all sorts of ribbons and trophies. I couldn't believe it—I've never won a trophy in my life!

"Did you win all of these?" I asked Jessie.

"About half of them," Jessie said. "Most of the ones for swimming are mine."

"From the camp we went to for three years," Pam stuck in. "Camp Ogunquit."

"And some of the baseball ones, too," Jessie went on as we headed up the stairs.

"Our camp baseball team was in first place two years in a row," Pam said proudly. "We were both Bluebirds."

"The rest of the trophies belong to my

brother, Michael," said Jessie. She pushed open the door to her room. "Just dump your stuff anywhere," she told us.

I had to be a little more careful with my bag than that, though. Besides my clothes, Jessie's birthday present was inside it.

Jessie has a terrific collection of glass horses. And for her birthday I had bought her a tiny crystal foal—that's a baby horse—with real gold inside its mane and tail.

"Dinner at six thirty," Mrs. Johnson called from downstairs.

Jessie glanced at the clock over her desk. "Great!" she said. "That gives us time to watch the video my granddad sent. Come on."

As we followed Jessie to the den, Pam asked, "What video?"

"Grandpop taped a gymkhana for me from the sports channel where he lives," Jessie explained. "I bet the Horizon Hills gymkhana will be just the same."

"What *is* a gymkhana, anyway?" Pam asked.

"Watch and see!" Jessie told her.

Gymkhanas are like field day games—on horses. The kids in the video seemed to be having lots of fun.

The first event was just like musical chairs—or musical horses! A bunch of kids trotted around a riding ring while music played in the background. When the music stopped, they jumped off their horses and scrambled to sit down on hay bales. Kids without bales were out of the game.

"Uh-oh. They have to remount without help," Pam pointed out anxiously.

One little girl pulled herself halfway onto her horse. But before she could throw her right leg over the saddle, her horse started trotting toward the gate. The girl lost her grip and ended up in the dirt!

"I'll really have to work at winning a blue ribbon in that event," Jessie said, shaking her head. "Ranger never stands still while I climb on."

17

Jessie's horse, Ranger, has a mind of his own.

"Wow, a sack race!" Pam said as the next event flashed on the TV screen.

A bunch of kids were jumping toward a finish line, their legs stuffed into big cloth bags. And as they jumped, the kids had to lead their horses behind them!

All three of us started laughing as we watched.

One boy was trying to stick his legs into a bag. But his horse didn't want to have anything to do with flapping cloth. The horse kept jerking away from him, pulling the reins out of the boy's hand.

A tall girl held her bag around her legs with one hand. Her other arm was hugging her horse's neck, and the horse was dragging her along. While she hung on for dear life, the horse pulled her right over the finish line!

"She won!" Pam cried. "Maybe I can do that."

18

"Gracie's probably the only one of our horses who is calm enough," Jessie agreed. "It's a good thing she's feeling better. Otherwise you wouldn't be able to ride her in the gymkhana."

Pam's horse, Gracie, is so calm that sometimes she dozes off in the middle of riding classes! No one had been able to figure out how Gracie managed to hurt herself recently. I had thought maybe she had dozed off and fallen down!

Next on the video was a relay race on horseback.

"Four kids on each team, just like us," Jessie said.

Unless I have to leave the group, I thought. *Then Jessie, Pam, and Peter won't even be able to enter this race!*

Jessie and Pam were laughing as they watched the kids racing their horses to a white pole and back. Instead of handing off sticks, the kids were using peeled bananas.

"Yuck! The banana's all mushy now and covered with dirt," Pam said, wrinkling her nose.

"Yeah, but if we don't drop it, we'll never have to dismount," Jessie pointed out. "Ranger is fast, and so is Winnie. There's no reason for us not to win this one, guys! And everybody gets a blue ribbon."

But if I'm an intermediate, no one gets a blue ribbon, I realized. *Jessie and Pam will never forgive me.*

The more I thought about it, the more sure I was. There was no way I could become an intermediate without making my friends mad at me. I had to convince Diana that I should stay in beginners.

So what should I do at Horizon Hills on Monday?

Ride my best?

Or ride my worst?

3

Jessie's birthday party started at ten o'clock the next morning at her house. Pam and I weren't the only girls invited, of course—Jessie's got tons of friends. So Libby Holman came, and Darla Sokel, and Janet Barton.

Libby has long, wavy reddish-blond hair and big blue eyes. She's one of the prettiest girls at school.

Darla is short, with curly brown hair. She's always kidding around and telling jokes. She makes everybody laugh.

Janet is quiet and more serious. She was

the lead in two school plays this past year.

Not one of them had said more than two words to me in the whole third grade.

But I had run into them at the mall this summer when I was there with Jessie and Pam. And we'd all had sundaes together at Burger Palace. I felt like they were starting to be my friends now, too. Maybe they had thought I was a snob in third grade, just like Jessie and Pam had.

When Darla, Libby, and Janet showed up at Jessie's on Saturday morning, they all seemed really happy to see me.

"Where do you get your hair cut?" Darla asked me. "It always looks great!"

And Libby said, "You were in the front yard when Janet and I passed by your house the other day."

"We yelled, but you didn't hear us," Janet added. "Maybe next time!"

I wanted to be happy that I had three new friends, but I couldn't stop thinking about pony camp, and moving to intermediate.

The trouble was, if Jessie and Pam didn't stay friends with me, Darla, Janet, and Libby wouldn't, either.

Mrs. Johnson drove us to the mall. The Johnsons belong to the health club there, and the six of us went swimming. Then we ate lunch at Taco Tamale—they have excellent chicken burritos. Mrs. Johnson had ordered an ice cream birthday cake ahead of time: fudge ripple and French vanilla, with a layer of chocolate chip cookies.

Jessie made a wish and blew out the ten candles—nine, and one to grow on.

"I wished that we win all the blue ribbons at the horse show!" she whispered to Pam and me.

Then Jessie opened her presents.

Pam gave her a braiding kit for horses, with a special brush, comb, and clips for braiding Ranger's mane and tail.

Janet and Darla together gave Jessie a silver bangle bracelet with galloping horses engraved on it.

"This is definitely the Year of the Horse," Mrs. Johnson said with a smile.

Libby gave Jessie a book called *Horses Around the World*.

But I think Jessie liked my present best.

When she unwrapped the glass foal, Jessie shrieked, "It's beautiful! Where did you get it, Maxine?"

"I saw one like it at the Westbrook Gallery," Libby said. "That's real gold inside the glass!"

"Wow!" said Jessie, stroking the foal's mane.

The other girls crowded around for a closer look.

"That's neat!" Janet said.

"Thanks a ton," Jessie said to me. "I love it!"

We ate most of the ice cream cake. Then we walked around the mall for an hour or so, and Mrs. Johnson drove us home.

Just before Libby got out of the car, she said to me, "Since we live near each other,

why don't you come over my house some-
time?"

"Great!" I said. "I will."

"Okay," said Libby. "I had a wonderful
time, Jessie. Bye!"

As we drove on, I watched Libby open
her front door. I couldn't believe it—I was
finally making friends!

My dad dropped me off at Horizon Hills early on Monday morning, on his way to work. He teaches electrical engineering at Jamestown Community College.

But even though I was early, I wasn't the first one at the barn. When I walked up the alley toward Winnie's stall, I noticed that Ranger's stall door was hanging open.

I poked my head in. And there was Ranger, all tacked up. (Tack is what you have to put on a horse in order to ride it— saddles and reins and stuff.) And there was Jessie, climbing into the saddle.

"Where's Diana?" I asked, glancing around. We aren't supposed to do any riding without an instructor.

"She's in the locker room," Jessie said. "She'll be here in a second."

Jessie climbed off Ranger. Then she pulled herself back up into the saddle again.

"What are you doing?" I asked her.

"Practicing getting on and off," Jessie said. Her feet hit the ground with a thump. Right away, she got ready to mount Ranger again.

Ranger is taller and rounder than Winnie. Jessie had to scramble up Ranger's left front leg to reach the saddle.

I saw Ranger's ears start to flatten against his neck.

In horses, flat ears are not a good sign. Flat ears mean the horse is losing patience.

Diana came up behind us. "Jessie, Ranger is getting annoyed," she said. "See how his ears are going back? I don't want to send you home with major teeth marks."

"Oh. Okay," Jessie said, looking surprised.

I giggled. Jessie has such a one-track mind that she hadn't even looked at Ranger's ears. The only thing she thought about was winning the relay race.

"Maxine," Diana said, "Mr. Morgan will be watching you this morning. Let's get Winnie tacked up."

"Why is Mr. Morgan watching Maxine?" Jessie asked.

But Diana had already started up the alley. I rushed after her so I wouldn't have to answer Jessie, either.

On the way we passed Peter standing outside Hogan's stall.

"Hello, Peter," Diana said. "Did you have a good weekend?"

Peter didn't say anything. He pressed his lips tightly together and frowned. Then he hurried into Hogan's stall.

"What's wrong with Peter?" Diana asked me.

I just shrugged. I had problems of my own to think about. I was going to have to fib about Mr. Morgan to Jessie and Pam. And I was going to have to fib *to* Mr. Morgan about my riding. I had to convince him that I wasn't as good as Diana thought I was.

"Maybe Mr. Morgan will have something better to do this morning than watch Maxine Brown," I said to Winnie as I tacked her up. "I mean, there are fifty-nine other kids at this camp!" Winnie looked doubtful.

Once our group had saddled our horses, we led them up the alley toward the door. We almost bumped into Lisa and Kevin Harris's intermediate group, coming from the other end of the alley.

Sally Keller swept past us as though we didn't exist. Bill Frano smiled at us before he walked on with his horse. Bill is the fourth kid in their group, and he's nice.

But Jessie was talking about the horse show, and Lisa must have overheard her.

"Thank your lucky stars that you're only beginners," Lisa said to Jessie. "If you had to compete with *real* riders, like us, you wouldn't win a single ribbon."

"Yeah, our dad is having a huge shelf built just for the trophies we'll bring home," Kevin added.

Then Kevin sneered at Peter. They are in the same grade at Jamestown Elementary, and Kevin never misses a chance to be rotten to Peter.

"So, Brody, how long are you going to have those train tracks in your mouth?" Kevin said with a snicker. Then he and Lisa led their horses out of the barn.

Peter's face was bright red. His lips were pressed even closer together.

"Braces!" Jessie and Pam whispered at the same time.

That's why Peter hadn't answered Diana. He hadn't wanted us to see his new braces!

"Peter, don't let Kevin get to you," I said.

"Besides," Jessie added, "we hadn't noticed

anything funny about your mouth."

"Oh, sure!" Peter mumbled, moving his lips just a tiny bit. "That's because I hadn't opened it!"

He looked ready to knock Kevin flat.

"I'll tell you what I almost wish. I almost wish we *were* intermediates. We'd beat the pants off them!" said Jessie, glaring at the Harrises' backs.

"Me too," Pam said.

"Yeah, well, I'd be perfectly happy to stay a beginner," I mumbled. I had just spotted Mr. Morgan heading toward the outside ring where we always ride. Diana was waiting for him at the gate, and they talked together for a moment before Mr. Morgan walked into the ring. He leaned against the fence, waiting.

There was no escape!

Diana held open the gate for the four of us and our horses. "This morning we're going to work on some of the skills you'll need for the gymkhana," she said. She smiled at Jessie. "I'm pretty certain that Ranger, at least, is tired of being mounted and dismounted."

Jessie nodded. "If *he* isn't, I sure am," she said. "My legs feel like they've taken a ten-mile hike up a mountainside!"

Diana gave Jessie a boost onto Ranger, then helped Peter, Pam, and me. As I settled myself in the saddle, I felt Mr. Morgan's eyes on me.

Good riders sit very straight. So I slumped down, trying to look as much like a bag of potatoes as possible.

"The events at the gymkhana will include a relay race," Diana said. "But instead of a baton, we'll be handing off a—"

"Banana!" Jessie cried.

"Are you a mind reader?" Diana asked, laughing.

"I have a videotape of a gymkhana," Jessie told her. "Pam, Maxine, and I watched it over the weekend."

"Great! Then you know what to expect.

I'll quickly explain it to Peter," Diana said, turning to him. "In this race, you hand off a banana to your teammates. But you have to be careful, because if it breaks, you have to get off your horse and pick up all the pieces of banana. Then you have to remount and give all the pieces to the next person!"

We heard a loud laugh. I turned around and saw Kevin Harris looking through the fence at us. "You're in serious trouble already!" he yelled. "How are you going to keep Peter from eating the banana before he crosses the finish line?"

It would have been kind of funny if it weren't so rotten. I mean, Peter *does* have a major appetite. When he sits with us at lunch, he usually ends up eating all of his own food, plus half of ours. But naturally, Peter doesn't like to be made fun of.

And he was furious! Two seconds after the words were out of Kevin's mouth, Peter had jumped off Hogan. He jerked his riding hat off his head and stormed over to the fence.

"I'm sick of you, Harris!" Peter bellowed at Kevin.

"Wow, major braces!" Jessie whispered to me, because Peter had finally opened his mouth wide.

Peter slammed his hat on the ground. He pushed the gate open, put up his fists, and said, "Come on, Harris!"

There hadn't been such excitement at Horizon Hills since Lisa Harris's horse lay down in the stream on the trail ride.

Kevin is taller than Peter, but he's skinny and kind of puny looking. With Peter right in his face, Kevin backed away fast—even before Diana and Mr. Morgan got between them.

"There is no fighting at Horizon Hills," Mr. Morgan said sternly. "Kevin, I want to talk to you in my office!"

"But I didn't do anything," Kevin whined.

"In my office!" Mr. Morgan repeated. "Now!" He was already striding through the gate.

Diana had picked up Peter's hat and was

brushing off the dirt. She handed it to him and said, "Peter, I know you had every reason to get angry. I would have been furious myself. But fighting with Kevin won't solve anything."

"I'm not so sure," Peter mumbled, his lips together again.

"It won't," Diana insisted, "and it's a good way to get kicked out of Horizon Hills." She went over to close the gate.

"Whenever Kevin or Lisa bothers me, I just remember something my dad always says," Jessie whispered to Peter. "'Success is the best revenge.'"

"What is that supposed to mean?" Peter asked.

"I think Jessie means get really good at riding," I said.

"Right! Win all the ribbons you can," said Jessie. "That will upset Kevin a lot more than fighting with him."

"And that goes for the rest of us, too," Pam chimed in. "Lisa will croak if we win more ribbons than they do."

"Let's go for it!" cried Peter.

Diana came back and helped Peter climb onto Hogan. We started practicing for the banana relay race.

Kevin didn't come back outside that morning.

Neither did Mr. Morgan, which solved one of my problems. I didn't have to make myself look bad on Winnie—at least for that day.

In fact, Jessie, Pam, Peter, and I were all totally psyched to win more ribbons than the Harrises at the gymkhana. We were terrific in practice!

And Diana had a surprise for us. She had brought along her video camera. She taped the whole lesson.

"This is exactly what professional riders do," she told us, squinting through the lens. "They watch their videotapes to see what they're doing wrong and what they're doing right."

Then Diana invited us to eat lunch with

her in Mr. Morgan's office and play back the tape on his VCR. Once we had bought sodas from the soda machine and un-wrapped our sandwiches from home, Diana turned on the VCR.

There was Jessie, trotting Ranger toward the white pole at the far end of the outdoor ring.

"This is cool!" Jessie said.

"Do you see anything you might improve about the way you're sitting in the saddle?" Diana asked her.

"But I had to do a sitting trot," Jessie ex-plained. "If I had tried to post, and hold on to the banana with one hand and the reins with the other, I would have ended up on my behind in the middle of the ring!"

"I agree with Jessie," I said.

"Yeah, a beginner would lose her balance if she were posting," Pam said. She sounded a little anxious just thinking about it.

"You're absolutely right; a sitting trot is the only way to do it," Diana said with a smile. "But Jessie, do you notice anything wrong with your feet?"

Jessie peered at the screen. "Is it that my feet aren't straight under my knees? They're a little too far back?"

Diana stopped the tape and pointed at Jessie's feet on the screen.

"Yup! Or right here, they're too far forward. *Feet* under *knees* under *thighs*," Diana said. "Tighten your thighs to grip the saddle a little harder. That will help you keep your balance."

One by one each of us flashed onto the screen: Jessie, Pam, and Peter. We all talked about what they were doing wrong, and what they were doing right.

I was last.

I watched myself holding a very yucky banana—it had already broken into three pieces by then—trotting to the white pole, then turning Winnie around the pole and trotting back.

"Anybody have anything to say about Maxine?" Diana asked us.

"She looked great," Pam said.

"Yeah, she did," said Jessie, and Peter nodded.

"Maxine, what do you think?" Diana asked me.

"I should have shortened the reins some more?" I asked.

"Well, maybe," said Diana. "But I think you looked pretty good. And I'll show this tape to Mr. Morgan, since he missed you in person this morning."

Oh, no! My stomach did another flip-flop.

"Why does Mr. Morgan want to look at Maxine?" Jessie asked, frowning a little.

"Diana . . ." I said softly, trying to stop her before she said anything else.

But Diana was already explaining. "I've told Mr. Morgan how well Maxine is riding," she said with a big smile. "And I've suggested to him that Maxine be moved into an intermediate group as soon as possible."

Jessie, Pam, and Peter all stopped chewing.

Slowly, the three of them turned to stare at me.

6

The five of us sat there for a couple of seconds, silent. Then Jessie, Pam, and Peter all spoke at once.

"You deserve it, Maxine," Jessie said.

"Congratulations!" cried Pam.

Even Peter mumbled, "Way to go, Max."

I couldn't believe it! I was upset, but they didn't even care that I would be moved out of their group! Jessie and Pam had said that all the intermediates were show-offs. They must think I'd fit right in.

"Which of the intermediate groups, Diana?" Pam asked.

"Mr. Morgan and I will take a good look at all of them," said Diana. "And then we'll decide."

"Is Maxine leaving us before the gymkhana?" Peter asked anxiously.

"Oh, no! We'd only have three people on our team—would we even be allowed to enter the relay race?" Jessie asked Diana. Jessie seemed more worried about winning her stupid ribbon than about losing me as a friend. . . .

"Maxine isn't going anywhere until after the horse show," Diana assured them.

"Lisa Harris will lose her teeth when she hears about this," Jessie said, grinning.

"Maxine won't get stuck with the Harrises, will she?" Pam asked.

This was worse than I expected. I hadn't even thought about the Harrises!

Diana was shaking her head. "I'll try to get Maxine into another group," she said.

"I'm really glad for you, Maxine," Pam said.

"I am, too," said Jessie.

They sound as though they mean it, I thought, surprised. Maybe everything was going to be okay. I would still see Jessie and Pam at lunch, and during afternoon activities, and on weekends. Or at least I hoped so.

It rained that afternoon, so we did crafts in the Little Red Barn. Jessie, Pam, and I sat at the same worktable, wood-burning designs onto coatracks.

With a super-hot wood-burning tool in your hand, you have to pay attention to what you're doing. The three of us weren't talking much.

But I did have something to ask them. "Uh . . . this Saturday is my birthday," I said, hoping they were still my friends. "And I was wondering . . ."

I expected Jessie to jump right in with a great birthday celebration idea. She usually loves planning things.

But she didn't.

Instead, Jessie and Pam glanced at each other.

Then Pam cleared her throat. "Um . . . Saturday?" she said in an odd voice.

"We're busy on Saturday," Jessie said quickly. "Remember, Pam?"

"Yeah. We have to go to . . . ah . . ." Pam mumbled.

"We have appointments at the Hair Studio for haircuts," Jessie said. "We've had them for ages."

Haircuts take the whole day? I thought.

"Yeah, and after that my grandmother is flying in from California—she's on her way to Europe—and we promised we'd show her around Westbrook," Pam continued.

"Yeah, she hasn't been here in—in ages. . . ." Jessie said, running out of steam.

The two of them sat there, looking very uneasy.

But I wasn't surprised. I knew this would happen when they found out I was becoming an intermediate—they already felt differently about me!

"What about Sunday?" I asked, just testing them.

"Sunday?" Pam repeated, giving Jessie a panicked look.

"Sunday is out, too," Jessie said immediately. "Pam's grandmother won't be leaving until Sunday afternoon, and we have to . . ."

"No big deal," I said, although I felt like dropping through the floor.

"Sorry," the two of them said together.

Jessie grabbed her wood-burning tool and started making stars all over her coatrack.

Pam picked up some sandpaper and sanded the edges of hers like crazy.

It was the *worst*! But I wasn't going to cry.

I had burned a horse head onto my coatrack—Winnie's head. Now I carefully burned curls into the curves of Winnie's mane. *So it's just Winnie and me again*, I thought.

Everything had changed.

I was still spending my days at Horizon Hills, of course. But Jessie and Pam were always watching me, and whispering together.

Peter never spoke. He even stopped eating. I guess his braces were bothering him.

And now that I was practically an intermediate, I couldn't seem to do anything right in the riding ring!

I squashed the banana twice in one morning when we were practicing for the relay race. Once I dropped it on the saddle while

Winnie was trotting. I sat on the banana before I could pick it up again. After that I tried so hard not to drop the banana that I mashed it flat against my favorite shirt.

When we practiced the sack race, I hopped too fast and fell down. Winnie almost stepped on me by accident.

Then Diana described another event that we'd be doing at the Horizon Hills gymkhana—apple bobbing. "You ride your horse as fast as you can to a bucket at the far end of the ring," she told us. "When you get there, you jump off, and you bob for an apple."

"I can't do it with my braces," Peter said crossly. "Or eat candy, or drink Cokes, or anything!"

Diana said Peter could sit out the apple bobbing, but Jessie, Pam, and I had to practice it. I've always been good at apple bobbing on Halloween. And if Jessie and Pam were going to treat me like an intermediate, I figured that I might as well act like one!

I cantered Winnie to the bucket, and I practically dove off her. Then I stumbled. My whole head went into the water up to my shoulders!

I came up coughing and spluttering in time to hear the Harrises laughing from the far end of the ring.

Diana rushed over to help me up.

"Are you okay, Maxine?" she asked. And she added in a lower voice, "Is anything bothering you?"

Just that I've lost the only friends I ever had! I was thinking. Of course, I didn't say it out loud. I just said, "Nothing's bothering me."

At home, my mom and dad kept asking me what I wanted to do for my birthday.

I kept saying, "I don't really care."

And I didn't. What good are birthdays without friends to help celebrate?

I didn't even care what my parents were *giving* me for my birthday. Usually I ask them millions of questions, trying to guess what my present is. Now I knew that nothing could make me feel better.

Jessie and Pam hadn't totally stopped talking to me. We had lunch together at Horizon Hills, as usual.

But they'd watch me out of the corner of their eyes. And they'd grin at each other, then stop as soon as I caught them at it. It was like they had secret thoughts they didn't want me to know about.

Usually the week flies by at Horizon Hills. I'm always sorry when Friday rolls around, because I won't be riding for two days. But that week seemed endless. I couldn't wait for it to be over!

I didn't feel any better, though, when I finally got home on Friday. In a few hours, I was going to be nine years old. And my parents still hadn't planned anything!

"So what are we doing tomorrow?" Dad asked cheerfully at the dinner table.

"I thought we might go shopping and pick out something for Maxine at the mall.

How about it, honey?" Mom asked me.

I couldn't believe it. They hadn't even bought my present yet. "Whatever you say," I answered glumly. It made no difference to me.

The next morning my dad brought me blueberry pancakes in bed on a tray, with a yellow rose in a little glass vase. He even sang "Happy Birthday," although he can't carry a tune.

My dad makes good blueberry pancakes. I didn't think I was hungry, but I ended up eating every bite. I stared at my plate in surprise. *Maybe I was just putting off starting my miserable birthday*, I thought. I got up and got dressed. Slowly.

"Maxine, come on," Mom called from downstairs.

"What's the hurry?" I grumbled. "It's not like I have any big plans."

But Mom and Dad hustled me into the car, and we rolled down the street. Then instead of turning right, toward the Westbrook Mall,

Mom turned left, heading out of town.

"I thought we were going to the mall," I said.

"Your mom and I thought the Jamestown Mall might be more fun," Dad said. "More stores. Anyway, I have to stop by Horizon Hills to drop off a check for the second half of camp."

I sighed and slumped down in the back-seat. *The second half of camp, when I won't have a friend in the world, except Winnie,* I thought. I didn't even look out the window when we turned into the long driveway and drove up to the barn at Horizon Hills.

Mom stopped the car. Dad opened his door. I didn't move.

"Aren't you coming with me, Maxine?" Dad asked. "You could say hello to Winnie."

"Oh, okay!" I muttered. After all, Winnie *was* my only friend.

I followed Dad into the barn. "That way," I said to him, pointing down the alley in the direction of Winnie's stall.

Without fifty or sixty kids running around, the barn was dead quiet, and kind of sad. I peered over stall doors at Gracie—she was dozing—and at Hogan, who was eating hay.

"This is it," I said over my shoulder to Dad.

I reached for Winnie's stall, unlatched the lock, and pulled the door open . . .

"SURPRISE!" five voices yelled at once. "Surprise, surprise!"

I almost fainted!

Jessie, Pam, Libby Holman, Darla Sokel, and Janet Barton were all inside Winnie's stall, screaming and jumping up and down!

"I can't believe it!" I said, screaming myself. "How . . . how did . . ."

"Your parents and Pam and I cooked up the whole thing last weekend!" Jessie said excitedly. "Pam and I have awful trouble keeping secrets. It was so hard not letting it slip out this past week!"

So that was why she and Pam had been acting so weird!

"And Darla and Janet and I thought a surprise party was a super idea!" Libby said. "*I* want to have one!"

"You can't have a surprise party for yourself," Janet pointed out sensibly.

All of us were so busy laughing that it took me a minute to realize that something was wrong. Winnie wasn't in her stall!

"Where is Winnie?" I asked Jessie. "Is she okay?"

A few weeks before, Pam's horse, Gracie, had hurt her leg. I wouldn't want something like that to happen to Winnie!

"She's right here, Maxine," said Dad.

He was standing in the alley with Winnie and Mom. Diana was there, too, with a big smile on her face.

"This is your birthday present from us, Maxine," Mom said.

"The surprise party?" I said. "I love it!"

"The surprise party," said Dad, "and the horse."

"What do you mean?" I asked.

Dad handed me the rope hooked to Winnie's halter. "We bought Winnie for you, Maxine—she's yours!" Dad said. "Happy birthday!"

8

Wow! I know it won't be possible to ever have a better birthday than my ninth, no matter how long I live!

For one thing, Winnie is mine now, all mine!

Which is terrific just because I love her, but also terrific for another reason. It means that we're never moving away from Westbrook. I mean, who could even *think* about moving around the world with a *horse*?

Plus, the party was wonderful. The six of

us had a great time! My parents had rented the side room at Burger Palace just for my birthday. There were banners and balloons and crepe paper strung up all over the place. There were even silly paper hats!

We played all the best songs on the juke-box. We stuffed down burgers and fries and onion rings. And my mom had bought a cake at Gleason's, the best bakery in Westbrook. It was white inside, with white icing and lemon filling—my favorite!

My presents were excellent, too. Jessie and Pam knew about me getting Winnie for my birthday, of course. So they had ordered a special halter for her from the Saddle Shop.

The halter was red, which was fabulous against Winnie's gray coat. WINNIE was painted in black on the nosepiece, and MAXINE BROWN was painted in smaller letters on the side. Everyone who saw Winnie would know she belonged to me!

Libby gave me a rhinestone pin in the

shape of a horseshoe. "For luck at all your horse shows with Winnie," she said.

Darla gave me a silver picture frame with hearts on it. "Maybe you can put a photo of all of us in it," she said. My dad was snapping hundreds of pictures of us at the party.

And Janet gave me a book called *Riding in the Olympics*. "Jessie says you're good enough to go to the Olympics yourself," Janet told me.

That pleased me at least as much as the present did!

After we had eaten the cake and ice cream, Mom and Dad drove us to the Water Park, on the other side of Jamestown. We stayed all afternoon, until we had gone on almost all of the rides.

On our way back to Westbrook, everybody agreed that this was the best birthday party ever!

I knew I had Jessie and Pam to thank for making it so perfect. When we were the only ones left in the car, I told them, "You guys were great for helping my parents plan all this."

"It was fun," Jessie said.

"That's what friends do," Pam added. "We were just afraid you were going to figure it out."

"Well, you *were* acting a little strange. But I thought you were mad at me about switching to intermediate," I admitted.

Jessie and Pam burst out laughing.

"What does that have to do with anything?" Jessie said. "Nothing will change, really. We'll still have lunch together every day and spend all our afternoons together," Pam added.

"And don't forget weekends," said Jessie.

"I won't!" I said.

Lunches, and afternoons, and weekends . . . and fourth grade, and fifth, and on and on!

What a wonderful birthday!

And you know how the week before my birthday I couldn't seem to do anything right during practice? Well, the week after my birthday, I couldn't seem to do anything wrong!

I'd always done well on Winnie. But now that she really belonged to me, we were super! The apple bob, the sack race, the relay—Winnie and I were unbeatable!

The rest of the group was having some problems that week. Practicing for the sack race, Gracie did let Pam grab her around the neck. But then, instead of pulling Pam over the finish line, Gracie walked slower . . . and slower . . . until she stopped altogether and closed her eyes!

"Gracie, how can we win if you fall asleep?" Pam groaned. And we were going to be out of luck during the relay race if Peter dropped the banana. He couldn't convince Hogan to let him get back in the saddle once he got out of it.

"Have you noticed? Peter isn't as big as he used to be," Pam pointed out as we watched Peter and Hogan chasing each other on Tuesday.

"Hey—you're right!" I said. "I think he's losing weight."

"Good for Peter! And good for the braces," said Jessie.

Her horse, Ranger, was afraid of the cloth bags in the sack race. Like the horse on the videotape, Ranger snorted, rolled his eyes, and flopped his head around. "And it's already Wednesday!" Jessie groaned. "We're running out of time!"

On Thursday, Diana gave all of us some useful tips.

"Peter, shorten your reins. Make your left rein even shorter than the right," Diana said. "That way, if Hogan starts walking, he'll have to turn to the left, toward you. And then you can climb on."

To Jessie she suggested, "Show Ranger the bag. Let him sniff it. You might even try sticking some apple slices in the bag. Then Ranger will think of tasty treats when he sees it, instead of getting scared.

"And Pam, maybe you could feed Gracie a couple of sugar cubes just before the gymkhana starts," Diana said. "Give her a little energy boost so she won't fall asleep."

And suddenly it was Friday!

9

Friday morning I jumped out of bed at six thirty to start getting ready for the gymkhana. First I braided my hair into a single braid. You're supposed to look as neat as you can for a horse show. I figured a braid would keep my hair out of my face.

Usually we just wear riding jeans, which are stretchy and comfortable. Riding jeans also have denim patches on the insides of the legs. The patches keep them from wearing out as fast as regular jeans, since they rub against the saddle all the time.

But horse shows are dressier than practice. So I put on my jodhpurs. They're cream-colored riding pants. They're stretchy, like the jeans. But they're looser at the hips, and tight from the knees down to the ankle. Because they fit snugly, you can really feel the horse under you.

Jodhpurs go with short jodhpur boots—the ones I always wear. On top, I wore a white blouse with a tie. And on top of that I wore a riding jacket, which looks like a blazer. For the fanciest horse shows, everyone is supposed to wear black jackets. And that happens to be the color of my jacket.

For horse shows—or anytime—the most important thing to wear is a riding hat. It keeps you from bashing your head if you fall off your horse. Mine is black velvet with a pink trim.

When I came down to breakfast, my dad said, "Maxine! You look ready to ride in the National Horse Show!"

"Oh, Dad!" I shook my head.

But I thought I did look pretty cool. And I was so excited!

Jessie and Pam were walking into the barn when we drove up, and they looked great, too. Both of them were wearing cream-colored jodhpurs. Pam was wearing a brown tweed jacket, and Jessie had on a black jacket like mine.

"Are you ready?" Jessie said to me.

"Ready for anything!" I said.

We weren't the only ones who had to look special for the show. The horses did, too.

With Diana's help and Jessie's new braiding kit, we braided our horses' manes and tails. I worked a red ribbon into Winnie's tail hair. Jessie used blue, and Pam green.

Even Peter got in on the braiding act. He did a really good job on Hogan's tail—without the ribbon. "Ribbons are for girls," he said.

"Hogan looks nifty," Diana said when Peter was finished. "And you do, too, Peter."

Peter was a little embarrassed, but I could tell he was pleased. "Yeah, I've dropped a few pounds," he mumbled.

He was wearing a dark gray tweed jacket with flecks of green and blue in it, and gray jodhpurs.

Diana checked her watch. "It's almost ten o'clock. Let's lead the horses out to the paddock." The paddock is the long pen in front of the barn. Our parents would be waiting there to cheer us on.

As we started out, the Harrises and Sally Keller were hurrying in.

"Hey, Lisa!" Jessie said. "I'll bet we win more ribbons than you guys do."

Lisa shrugged. "Even if you do, it won't mean anything. We're intermediates. You're only competing against babies." She sniffed.

Kevin and Sally laughed, and the three of them turned into the alley.

"They burn me up," Jessie said, scowling after them.

"That goes double for me," said Peter.

"Just remember what Jessie's dad says," Pam reminded us. "'Success—'"

"'—is the best revenge!'" Jessie, Peter, and I finished.

"Let's go get 'em!" Peter added, punching his fist in the air.

There were lots of people gathered around the paddock. It looked like everyone's parents had taken time off from work to come to the horse show. And there were sisters and brothers—I saw Jessie's brother, Michael—and grandparents, too, leaning against the fence or sitting in lawn chairs.

I'd never ridden Winnie in front of a crowd before. All of those people seemed to pump her up. She bobbed her head and stamped her feet.

"The beginners will compete first, then intermediates," Mr. Morgan announced over a microphone. "And last, our instructors will put on a jumping demonstration!" Everybody cheered.

"The first event is a lot like musical

chairs," Mr. Morgan continued. "There are twenty-eight beginners—too many for just one round. So we've divided them into two groups."

I was glad that Mr. Morgan read out our names in the first group, because Winnie was ready to go!

"Please mount your horses and line up," Mr. Morgan said.

Diana helped us get mounted and settled in the saddle. We lined up with Jessie first, behind a tall, dark-haired boy. Pam edged in after Jessie, I was next, and Peter behind me.

"These are the rules: When the music stops, anyone who ends up without a hay bale to sit on is out of the event," boomed Mr. Morgan. "Also, if it takes you longer than a minute to remount your horse, you're out of the event."

I heard Peter groan behind me. I knew he was worried about climbing on and off Hogan.

"We'll be starting out with fourteen riders

and thirteen hay bales," Mr. Morgan said.

The hay bales had been laid out in a circle in the middle of the paddock. The music started. We rode around the hay bales once . . . twice . . . and the music stopped!

Since I was jumping off Winnie to get a hay bale for myself, I didn't have a chance to watch the others. But once I was safely sitting on a bale, I looked around. All four of us had made it!

And Hogan stood as still as a statue for Peter to climb back on him—from the top of the hay bale!

"Good idea, Peter!" Jessie said, climbing onto her own hay bale to remount Ranger.

Pam was out of the game on the third or fourth round. She got pushed aside by a short girl with two braids and a very strong shove.

Jessie stubbed her toe on the ground on the eighth round and got beaten to a hay bale. She was out.

I made it almost to the end.

It was just me, Peter, and the tall boy who had ridden next to Jessie, and two hay bales. The music stopped when the tall boy and I were in front of the same hay bale. His legs were so long that he took just one step off his horse and one step over to the hay bale. He was practically sitting on the hay before I'd even jumped off Winnie!

I was out.

I led Winnie to the fence, where Jessie and Pam were waiting for me with Diana.

"You still win a white ribbon, Maxine, for third," Pam said.

"I just hope Peter wins first," I told them.

We watched as Peter and the tall boy rode around and around the last hay bale.

"I can't watch," Pam said, covering her eyes.

Suddenly the music stopped!

Peter and the other boy jumped off their horses . . .

"It's not fair—he's twice as tall as Peter!" Jessie said.

But the toe of the tall boy's boot caught on Hogan's back leg!

"He's falling!" Diana cried.

"Who—Peter?" said Pam, her eyes still covered.

But Jessie and I were screaming, "Peter won! Peter won!"

Peter patted his blue-ribbon hay bale, looking very pleased with himself.

I placed second in the apple bob. Jessie and Pam placed third and fourth! Peter had to sit that one out because of his braces. But he said he didn't mind now that he had his blue ribbon.

And Pam won the sack race—with Gracie's help! Maybe all the cheering from the crowd forced Gracie to stay awake. Anyway, she dragged Pam across the finish line pretty fast, before Jessie and Peter and I were even halfway to it.

Finally our big moment came. It was time for the banana relay race!

10

The four of us had decided that Jessie would go first in the relay, Pam would go next, then Peter, and me last, because Winnie is the fastest.

We would be racing at the same time as one other team. But even if we beat that team, we wouldn't know if we had won ribbons until all seven beginner teams had raced.

Mr. Morgan and one of the instructors would be timing every team with stopwatches.

"Just take it easy," Diana told us. "Really

grip that banana hard. You don't want to drop it—you'll lose too much time getting off your horse to pick it up."

All of us gripped our banana, all right. Nobody dropped it. And by the time Peter passed it to me, it was practically *banana sauce*!

I didn't care. I mashed it up against me and got Winnie going in a canter. I barely slowed down for the end pole, made a tight circle around it, and raced back across the finish line!

I stopped Winnie and pulled my hand away from my jacket. I had gooey banana smeared all across my blouse!

"Yuck!" I said.

But my team was yelling, "Way to go, Maxine!"

We had beaten the other team by two or three horse lengths!

Of course, five more teams still had to run. And some of them looked like they were really fast.

Finally the last member of the last team crossed the finish line.

"That completes the beginners relay race, ladies and gentlemen," Mr. Morgan announced. "If you'll just give us a moment, we will look at the numbers and figure out who the winners are."

Jessie, Pam, and I all crossed our fingers and held our breath. Peter made the "V" sign, for "victory."

Finally Mr. Morgan stepped up to the microphone again. "The fourth-place winners for the relay are . . ." And Mr. Morgan read out four names that weren't ours.

There was cheering and clapping from the audience.

Then Mr. Morgan read out the names of the third-place winners.

"Whew! Not us, either," said Jessie, relieved.

The second-place winners were the team with the tall boy from musical hay bales.

"He's winning another second-place ribbon," Pam said. "Not bad!"

Now all four of us were really nervous. We hadn't really wanted to win third or fourth in the relay. But what if we didn't place at all?

Mr. Morgan cleared his throat and spoke into the microphone: "And the blue-ribbon winners of the beginners relay are . . ." He paused just long enough for all of us to stop breathing totally. "The winners are . . . Jessie Johnson, Pam Werner, Peter Brody, and Maxine Brown!"

I know our parents were clapping. But I couldn't hear them because we were all screaming so loud, and jumping up and down!

Diana finally had to tell us to settle down, because we were making our horses crazy. But she had been jumping up and down right along with us!

"A blue ribbon to add to my collection!" Jessie said proudly.

"I've never won a blue ribbon before," I said.

"Neither have I," said Peter.

"And now you've got two!" Diana pointed out to him.

"Remember what I told you?" Jessie said.

"Yeah. Success *is* the best revenge!" Peter said proudly.

"Kevin Harris will absolutely croak!" Pam giggled.

"Lisa, too," Jessie added. "Although I guess she'll say they're just *baby* blue ribbons."

That's when an intermediate girl walked up to our group. She was about my height, with long black hair pulled back in a ponytail and green eyes.

"Diana?" she asked. "Can I talk to you for a second?"

"Sure, Kirsten," said Diana. "Group, this is Kirsten Rogers—one of the intermediate riders. Kirsten, this is Jessie, and Pam, and Peter . . . and this is Maxine."

As Kirsten said hello to all of us, Diana added, "Maxine, you'll be the fourth member of Kirsten's group, starting next week."

"So soon?" I said. I felt a little sad. But I also felt excited.

Kirsten smiled at me. "Maybe sooner," she said. Then she asked Diana, "We wondered if we could borrow Maxine for today. With only three for the relay, one of us will have to run twice, unless Maxine fills in as fourth."

"Maxine riding as an intermediate?" Jessie exclaimed. "Wow! Stick that in your ear, Lisa Harris!"

All of us started laughing, even Kirsten. I guess the Harrises aren't any more popular with the intermediates than they are with beginners!

Diana said, "If it's okay with Maxine— and Mr. Morgan—I don't see why she shouldn't."

And that's how I ended up running in the intermediate relay with my new team: Kirsten Rogers, Hannah Paulsen, and Wesley Sykes.

It just happened that the team running against us was the Harrises'. I thought their eyes would bug out when they saw me!

But better than that . . . we beat them!

Kirsten went first, then Wesley, then me, and last Hannah. I almost dropped the banana and had to slow down to get a better grip on it. But Hannah rides a very fast black horse named Ebony. She practically flew to the pole and back! She crossed the finish line miles before Kevin Harris did.

I could hear Jessie, Pam, and Peter yelling their heads off on the sidelines. But when Mr. Morgan announced the blue-ribbon winners, they shouted until they were hoarse!

"The winners of the intermediate relay are . . . Kirsten Rogers, Wesley Sykes, Hannah Paulsen, and I believe that's Maxine Brown again. She's our newest intermediate!"

Kirsten, Hannah, and Wesley were shouting, too.

"We won!" Wesley yelled. "Good work, Maxine!"

"Glad you're with us," Kirsten told me.

And Hannah added, "We're going to make a great team!"

She and Kirsten gave me a big hug.

It was even better than my birthday. New friends, old friends, and two blue ribbons! I couldn't ask for more!